The Hopes and Dreams Series
Italian-Americans

Littl Italy

A story based on history

Second Edition

Tana Reiff

Illustrations by Tyler Stiene

PR◌ LiNGUA
LEARNING

Pro Lingua Learning

PO Box 4467, Rockville, Maryland 20849
Office: 1-301-242-8900, Book orders: 1-800-888-4741
Web: ProLinguaLearning.com
Email: Info@ ProLinguaLearning.com

Print Edition ISBN 978-0-86647-389-7

The first edition of this book was originally published by Fearon Education, a division of David S. Lake Publishers, Belmont, California, Copyright © 1989, later by Pearson Education. This, the second edition, has been revised and redesigned.

The cover and illustrations are by Tyler Stiene. The book was set and designed by Tana Reiff, consulting with A.A. Burrows, using the Adobe *Century Schoolbook* typeface for the text. This is a digital adaptation of one of the most popular faces of the twentieth century. Century's distinctive roman and italic fonts and its clear, dark strokes and serifs were designed, as the name suggests, to make schoolbooks easy to read. The display font used on the cover and titles is a 21st-century digital invention titled Telugu. It is designed to work on all digital platforms and with Indic scripts. Telugu is named for the Telugu people in southern India and their widely spoken language. This is a simple, strong, and interesting sans serif display font.

Audio MP3 files for this book are available for purchase and download at ProLinguaLearning.com/audio.

The Hopes and Dreams Series
by Tana Reiff

The Magic Paper (Mexican-Americans)
For Gold and Blood (Chinese-Americans)
Nobody Knows (African-Americans)
Little Italy (Italian-Americans)
Hungry No More (Irish-Americans)
Sent Away (Japanese-Americans)
Two Hearts (Greek-Americans)
A Different Home (Cuban-Americans)
The Family from Vietnam (Vietnamese-Americans)
Old Ways, New Ways (Jewish-Americans)
Amala's Hope (A Family from Syria)
Neighbors (A Family from El Salvador)

Contents

1 Hard Times in Italy

Southern Italy, 1920

"Little ones!"
said Rosetta.
"Your Papa is home!
Let's clean you up.
I want you
to look pretty
for your Papa."

The three children
came to their mother.
She washed
their six little hands.
Then she returned
to the pot of sauce
on the stove.

Vito Trella
opened the door.
The door was broken.
It made a loud noise.
Vito did not look happy.

"So sad, so sad,"
he said,
shaking his head
from side to side.

"You know how
to fix the door,"
Rosetta said.

"No, no, not that,"
said Vito,
rubbing his head.
"The trouble
is not the door.
The door
is easy to fix.
The trouble
is the fruit.
I cannot sell
enough oranges.
I don't know
how to fix that."

"What is wrong
with the oranges?"
asked Rosetta.
"They taste sweet to me."

"The sweetest oranges
in the whole world!"
said Vito.
"But the Americans
do not need oranges
from Italy anymore.
They grow oranges
in North America now.
And our land
is wearing out.
We do not get
as many oranges
as we did before.
They are small, too."

"What shall we do?"
asked Rosetta.

"We must think about
going to another place,"
said Vito.
"We must think about
going to America.
Our land is poor.
Our town is crowded.
Everyone is poor.

Our children
will have nothing
if we stay here.
They need a chance
for a better life.
That is the best gift
we could ever give them."

"I want that too,"
said Rosetta.
"But a new life in America?
It would be so different."

"We could make
a better living,"
said Vito.
"We cannot make
a good living here.
We could give
our children
hope for tomorrow."

"Do we have
enough money
to go to America?"
asked Rosetta.

"We have enough
to buy one ticket,"
said Vito.
"I will go first.
I will work hard
and save money.
I will send you money
to buy tickets.
Then you can bring
the children over."

Rosetta hated to see
her husband go away.
She did not want
to leave her town.
She did not want
to take the children
to America
by herself.
But she knew
Vito's plan
might be the only way
to make things better.

2   A Ship to America

Rosetta and Vito
saw the signs
all around town.
Ships were looking
for people
to take to America.
Once a week,
a young man
came to town.
He sold tickets
to ride on a ship.
He talked about
the streets of gold
in America.

For months,
Rosetta helped Vito
get ready for the trip.
She packed
a bag for him.
She packed salted meat,
bread, and cheese.
She packed
his clothes.

Her tears
fell on the bag.
Those tears
would go to America,
along with her husband.

All the neighbors
came to say goodbye.
They waved and cried.
They kissed and hugged.
They wished Vito
good luck and good health.

Then Vito turned
to his family.
"Goodbye, my loves,"
he said.
"I will write to you.
I will send money.
The four of you
will come to America
very soon."

In his mind,
Vito said goodbye
to his town, too.
He had lived here
all his life.

He would miss
his farm.
It had once been
a good farm.
He looked back
at the mountains.
He had loved
to climb those mountains.
He remembered
the river.
He had loved
to swim and fish
in that river.
He was leaving
everything he knew
and everyone he loved.

He tried
to act brave.
He hugged his family
one last time.
His heart was full
of love and fear.

A horse cart
took Vito and his bag
to the train station.
The train
took him to Naples.
There, he saw
the big ships.
On the dock
he bought a book.

The book cover said,
"Learn English
by the time
you reach New York!"

Vito laughed.
But he bought
the book anyway.

A ship's mate
tied a little tag
to his coat.
On the tag
were his name
and some numbers.

Then Vito
and the other people
got in line.
The ship's mates
pushed the people
up a ramp
to board the ship.
Vito felt
like a farm animal.

The ship
was on the ocean
for 15 long days.
Finally, the trip was over.
Vito was in New York.
He was in America.

3 New York

Vito found
a place to live
in New York.
He did not have money
to go any farther.
There was work here,
so he stayed
in the city.

But the work
was not farm work.
Vito took a job
as a stone worker.
He learned to cut
blocks of stone.
He lifted them
into place.
One by one,
the stones grew
into tall buildings.
Many new buildings
were going up
in New York
at that time.

They were called "skyscrapers"
because they seemed
to touch the sky.

It was very hard work.
Dangerous work.
But every day
was one day closer
to seeing his family.
Every day
was one day closer
to a better life.
Vito tried not to think
about the hard work.
He could only think about
how happy he would be
to see his family.

After work,
Vito was alone.
He ate dinner,
but it was never as good
as his wife's cooking.
After dinner,
he read and studied.

He learned
some English
from the little book
he had bought
in Naples.

He lived
on very little.
He saved
almost all his money.

Vito worked
with a man
named Sal Penta.
Sal was also
from Italy.

"Come out with us!"
said Sal one day.
"We have a good time!
Meet us tonight
at the bar."

Vito did not like bars.
But he went there
for something to do.

A group of men
were playing cards and
drinking.
There was money
on the tables.
There were pretty women
waiting for the men.

"How much
have you won?"
Vito asked Sal.

"Fifty dollars so far!"
Sal laughed.
"Come on, give it a try!"

Vito watched.
He did not want
to join the game.

"What's the matter?"
Sal asked him.
"It's easy money!
Are you chicken?"

"I don't want
to bet any money,"
Vito told him.
"I'm saving up
to bring my family over."

"So am I!"
said Sal.
"Come on, Trella!"

Vito slowly sat down
at the card table.
"All right,"
he said.
"I'll give it a try."

It was a lucky night
for Vito Trella.
By the time
the game was over,
he had won
more than $100.

The next week,
Vito went back
to the bar
to play cards.

This time,
he was not so lucky.
He lost
all of his money.
Sal and the others
lent him more.
But Vito
lost all of that too.

Later that night,
Vito lay awake
in his bed.
He could not sleep.

"How could I do
such a thing?"
he asked himself.
"All the money
I have saved
is gone.
All of it!
Gone."

He felt sick.
He told himself
he would pay back
the money he borrowed
from his friends.
And then
he would never again
play cards.

It took two years
to save enough money
for four tickets
to America.

Vito sent the money
home to Italy.
Then he waited
to see his family again.
Sal Penta's family
was still waiting.

4 Two Bags

"Who is the man
in that picture?"
asked little Felice.

"That is your Papa,"
Rosetta said.
"You don't remember him,
do you, my kitten?"

"No, Mamma,"
said little Felice.

"You were very young
when your father
went to America,"
said Rosetta.
"But you will know him.
Believe me,
my little kitten.
Papa will send us money
to go to America.
It will be soon."

Rosetta tried to believe
her own words.
But hundreds of days
had gone by
without her husband.
His letters
were special,
but not enough.
She tried
to keep up the farm.
Her son Pino
helped out.
But he was
just a child.
Sometimes Rosetta
lost heart.
Would she and the children
ever go to America?

Then one day
the money came.
"My dear family,"
Vito wrote.
"At last!
I have been without you
for more than two years.

Now it is time
to begin our life together
in America.
Come and join me
as soon as you can.
Love, Papa."

"Children, children!
We are going
to America!"
cried Rosetta.
"We will be
with Papa again!"

Pino smiled.
But to little Felice
and her sister Angela,
their father
was just a picture.

"Let's dance!"
said Rosetta.
She and the children
joined hands.
They danced in a circle.
The little girls
began to laugh.

Rosetta sold
almost everything.
She packed two bags
for the trip.
One bag
held clothes and food.
The other bag
held memories of the past
and hope for tomorrow.
She carried
that second bag
in her mind.

Like Vito before her,
she and the children
went to Naples
to board a ship.
Now they too
were on their way
to a new life.

5   Across the Ocean

The trip
across the ocean
was very hard.
The ship was packed
full of people.
The Trellas stayed
under the deck,
where tickets cost less.
There were no windows.
It was dark down there.
Days were hot.
Nights were cold.
The children cried.
"Be still,"
Rosetta told her children.
"Soon we will be
in America.
Everything
will be all right."

"Take a walk
up on the deck,"
a woman said to Rosetta.

Her name was Mrs. Santo.
"Get some fresh air.
I will watch
your children."

Mrs. Santo
was taking
her two children
to America
by herself.
Her husband was dead.

The five children
played together
every day.
They played games.
They sang songs.

"I hope
we will be friends
in America,"
said Rosetta.

"I hope so too.
Let's stay in touch,"
said Mrs. Santo
as she rubbed her eye.

"What is wrong
with your eye?"
Mrs. Trella asked.

"Maybe some dust
flew into my eye,"
said Mrs. Santo.

Her eye was red.
It looked like
it was on fire.
As the days went on,
Mrs. Santo's other eye
got red, too.
Her eyes hurt
during the whole trip
across the ocean.
She touched
no one on the ship
but her own children.

6　A New Day

They had been at sea
for 15 days.
A bad storm
had lasted for days.
They felt sick
and could not eat.
Rosetta had prayed,
day and night.
Almost everyone
felt tired and weak.
But this morning
everyone felt happy.

"Get ready!"
a man on the ship
called out.
"We're almost there!"

The sun
was just coming up.
A light pink sky
was opening up
a new day.

"Wake up!"
Rosetta said
to the children.
"We are almost
in America!"

Everyone on board
clapped and cheered.
They ran
up to the deck.
They hung
over the rail
to see better.
All the parents
lifted up their children.
Everyone wanted
to see New York City.

Rosetta was the first
to spot land.

"There it is!"
she cried.
"I see America!
Oh, look!
The Statue of Liberty!"

She held Felice
in her arm.
She pointed
to the statue
in the water.
"Can you see
that beautiful lady?"

The Statue of Liberty
seemed to stand
on the water.
The huge lady
held a torch of fire
in one hand.
The sun
made her crown shine.
Without a word
she seemed to say,
"Welcome to America!
You are safe with me."

Rosetta knew
she would never forget
this sight.

"Look, children!"
she said.
"Look at the buildings
behind the lady!
What a beautiful city!
Just as Papa
wrote in his letters!
He helped to build
those tall buildings,
you know."

"It looks like
a story book!"
said little Felice.

The ship
pulled into a large dock.
Right away,
the rich people
walked off the ship.

"Don't rush out!"
a man called
to everyone else.

"Get into a boat
over there.
You must go
to Ellis Island.
They will check you over.
Then you will be able
to go into the city."

When the boats
got to Ellis Island,
Vito was waiting.
He lifted up
his wife.
They held each other.
They jumped
up and down.
Then he picked up
all three children.
He had
a wide smile
on his face.
This was
a very happy morning.

7   Ellis Island

Rosetta and the children
went into the big building
on Ellis Island.
They stood
in a long line of people
from the ship.
They waited
almost all day.
Mrs. Santo and her children
stood in front of them.
Vito waited
in another room.

At last, the Santos
got to the head
of the line.

A large woman
looked the Santo children over.

"They look fine,"
she said.

Next, she looked
Mrs. Santo over.
She saw
the red eyes.
She lifted
Mrs. Santo's eyelids
with a long hook.
"Your eyes
look very bad,"
said the woman.
"We cannot let
sick people
into the country.
We don't want anyone
to catch your sickness.
I am sorry.
We must send you
back to Italy."

"What did she say?"
Mrs. Santo asked.
A man who spoke
English and Italian
told her.

"Go back to Italy?"
cried Mrs. Santo.
"After such a long trip?
I must turn around
and go back?
How can this be?
Please let us stay!
My eyes
will get better!"

"God be with you,"
said Rosetta.
She felt very sad
for the Santo family.

A man
took Mrs. Santo
by the arm.
He took the family
to a boat.
The Santos
would never set foot
in New York City.

Then came
Rosetta's turn.
The large woman
checked her over.

Then she checked
each child.
She put strong drops
into their eyes.
She pulled their hair.
"That hurts!"
cried little Felice,
holding her head.

"You may move on,"
the large woman said.

"Oh, thank you!"
said Rosetta in Italian.

Next, a young man
asked Rosetta
many questions,
"Where were you born?
Where did you live?
Are you married?
Do you know anyone
in America?
Where are you going?
Have you ever
broken the law?
How much money
do you have?

The questions
were hard
because Rosetta
did not speak English.
She tried
to understand.

"You have passed
all the tests,"
said the young man.
"You may move on."
He gave her
some papers.
She held the papers
close to her body.

A boat
took all five Trellas
over to the city.
They could see
the Statue of Liberty
grow smaller
behind them.
Rosetta was the first one
to get off the boat.
She watched her foot
touch the ground.

"Are we really here?"
she asked her husband.

"You really are
in America!"
said Vito.
"We really are
together again.
Our new life
begins today!"

8 Together Again

The Trella family
walked together
into the city.
Rosetta could not
believe her eyes.
New York
was nothing like Italy!
Some buildings here
were 40 stories high.
No high buildings
back home!
The streets here
were wide and dirty.
They were not
made of gold,
as people back home said.

Vito took the family
to their new home.
The tiny apartment
was in a big building
on Mulberry Street.

The family would live
in two small rooms,
five floors above the street.
In the same building
lived 20 other families.
Rosetta looked
for windows.
There were none.
The place was dirty.
And it was hot.

"What is wrong?"
asked Vito.
"You did not think
we would live
in a grand house,
did you?"

"No, no,"
said Rosetta.
"This is all right.
We will make do
with what we have.
You will see!
I will make
these two rooms
clean and pretty."

And so she did.
She cleaned up
the two little rooms.
She hung up sheets
between the beds.
She made two rooms
into a home.
Oil lamps gave some light.
When the place was hot,
the family went out
and sat on the fire escape.

Vito worked hard
12 hours a day.
He was always dirty
when he came home.
Many times,
he was hurt
from cutting stones.

Rosetta looked
at her husband.
She looked up
at the tall buildings.
He was helping
to build them.
She saw her husband's pain
in those skyscrapers.

      She spent
her days and nights
helping her family.
Her job
was to make a home.
Life was not easy.
But the family
was in America.
Together again.
That was
the only thing
that mattered.

9 Mulberry Street

The Trella family
went to church together
every Sunday.
Rosetta went by herself
almost every day.
She met many people
at church.

The rest of the time,
Rosetta and the children
spent many happy hours
on Mulberry Street.
It was like a street fair
all the time.
Rosetta talked
with her neighbors.
Most of them
were from Italy.
Rosetta and Vito
even knew a few of them
from back home.

She loved
being with people
from the "old country."
They spoke
to each other
in Italian.

No one had a place
to store food
or keep it cold.
So they went shopping
on the street.
Men pushed carts
through the street
early every morning.
They sold fresh food
off the carts.

Rosetta picked out oranges
from one of the carts.
They were not as sweet
as the ones back home.
But she still loved oranges.

Next, she picked out
fresh vegetables.
She bought
her meat or fish last.
She didn't want anything
to go bad
while she talked
with her friends.

All the children
played in the street.
They ran around
in between the carts.
They laughed and sang
and played games.
Sometimes they
got into fights.
But mostly
they had fun.

Rosetta knew
that the children
were safe on the street.
She could cook and clean
so much faster
when they were
out of the way.

She went down
to get them
when it was time
for dinner.

With so many Italians
and street markets,
New York felt like home.
That is why
people called
this part of the city
"Little Italy."

10 Building a Life

Over the next five years
Vito and Rosetta
had four more children.
Now there were seven.

First there was Pino.
His real name
was Giuseppe.
In America
people called him Joe.
Next came the two girls,
Felice and Angela.

The last four
were born in New York.
The two boys
were Pasquale and Guido.
Then came Annalia,
the youngest girl.
The last child
was a boy.
His name
was Dominick.

The family of nine
still lived in two rooms.
It was crowded.
But they were together.

Rosetta took care
of the seven children.
She cooked
three meals a day.
She always had
a pot of sauce
on the stove.
She kept the apartment
clean and neat.
If Rosetta was awake,
she was busy.

The Trella children
never had new clothes.
There was no money
for store-bought clothes.
Rosetta made everything.
The old clothes
were handed down
from one child to the next.
If something had a hole,
Rosetta fixed it.

"We cannot
throw away clothes,"
she told the children.
"Your clothes
may be old.
But they
always will be clean.
My children
always will look neat.
No one will know
that we live
in two little rooms."

But one day
Dominick came home
from school
with torn pants.
He was crying.

"You're a big boy,"
said his mother.
"Why are you crying?"

"I got into a fight,"
the boy said.

"Why?"

"The other boys
make fun of me,"
said Dominick.
"They call me names.
They say
I wear funny clothes.
They tell me
I am not American.
I didn't like them
saying those things.
So I hit them."

"You were born
in this country,"
Rosetta said.
"You are American.
The day will come
when you will have
new clothes.
But now you don't.
And I don't want you
to fight about it."

"But the other boys
make me feel bad,"
said Dominick.

"Don't listen to them,"
said Rosetta.
"You are a good boy.
I want you to be
the best you can be."

11 Lucky To Be Alive

Vito was working
on a big new building
on 58th Street.
He stood
on a board
near the top
of the building.
The board hung
from two ropes.
Another board
lifted stones
from the street
up to Vito.
His job
was to put the stones
in place.

"Two more loads!"
shouted the boss.

The next-to-last load
came up to Vito.

"Get that board closer!"
Vito called back in English.
"I can't reach it!"

"Not too close!"
a man on the ground
called out.
"You don't want
to hit the building!"

Vito reached
for a stone.

"You almost have it!"
shouted the boss.

Vito reached out more.
Then suddenly,
the board full of stones
dropped ten feet.
Vito tried
to grab a rope.
The board
was too far away.
Vito grabbed only air.
His foot slipped.
A wave of fear
ran through his body.

"Watch out!"
he heard someone say.
But it was too late.
Vito fell
off his board.
He landed
on the other board,
on a pile of stones.

All the other men
stopped working.
"Hold on tight!"
the boss called to Vito.
"We're bringing you down."

Vito could not understand
the boss's English.
He just held on
to the rope
for dear life.

Down came
the load of stones.
Slow, slow, stop.
The board with the stones
hit the street.

Vito rolled off
the board.
He lay on his back
on the street.

"Are you all right?"
the boss asked.
"What hurts?"

"My back,"
Vito said in Italian.

The boss
did not understand
Vito's Italian.
"He hurt his leg,"
the boss said.

Vito tried
to stand up.
The boss came over
to help him get up.

"Go home,"
the boss said.
"Come back tomorrow
when you feel better."

But the next day,
Vito did not feel better.
He couldn't walk.
He could only feel
a sharp pain
in his back.
But he felt lucky
just to be alive.

12   Paper Flowers

Vito never went back
to stone work.
He could walk,
but his back hurt
all the time.

He found work
making paper flowers.
The pay was very low.
But it was the only work
he could do.
The little shop
was on the first floor
of a building
a few blocks away.
There were apartments
on the upper floors.

The Trella family
moved into the building.
Now they had
three rooms instead of two.

They had two windows.
Still, the apartment
was small for nine people.

The whole family
helped to make
paper flowers.
And every night,
the children studied.
"Very important
to do well in school,"
Rosetta told them.
"I want you
to make something
of your lives."

When she left Italy,
Rosetta packed
two bags.
One was real.
One was in her mind.
Every day,
Rosetta looked
into the bag
in her mind.
It was full
of memories and hope.

That bag
was fuller now
than it had ever been.

She and her neighbors
talked about the old country.
All of the women
had high hopes
for their children.
They loved to talk.
Their whole world
was Mulberry Street.
Little Italy
was the only America
that they knew.

And so, around that time,
the five Italian-born Trellas
became U.S. citizens.
From then on,
the Trella family
were true Italian-Americans.

13   Festa!

Summer was the time
for the church festa.
It was very much like
any festa back in Italy.
People carried
tall candles
through the street.
They pinned dollar bills
to the church door.
They hung strings
of colorful lights.
They hung
flowers and flags.
They played games
and ate lots of food.
After dark,
they set off fireworks.
They sang and danced
in the street.
Vito and Rosetta danced.
Vito didn't care
if his back hurt.

"We should dance
more often,"
he said.

"When would we dance?
Rosetta laughed.
"We are always busy
with the family."

"Our children
are growing up,"
said Vito.
"Soon there will be
just you and me again."

"I miss Felice,"
said Rosetta.
"My little kitten."

"Felice is fine!"
said Vito.
"She has given us
beautiful grandchildren."

"I thank God,"
said Rosetta.
"I hope we will have
many more!"

"And look at Joe!
He is doing so well,"
Vito said.
"He lives uptown,
in a nice apartment.
He works
in an office.
He has a fine wife.
I am happy for him."

"Pasquale and Guido
are building skyscrapers,"
said Rosetta.
"Just like you did.
They work hard.
They are doing well.
They even help to run
the building company!"

"And Angela and Annalia
work in a clothing factory."
said Vito.
"They will marry one day.
Then they too will be gone."

"I can't believe
our little Dominick
is in high school,"
said Rosetta.
"Time goes by
so fast."

As they were talking,
the music got louder.
"My favorite song!"
Vito said.
He grabbed
his wife's hand.
"Let's dance all night!"

14 Top of the Class

The years went by.
Dominick was
the only child
still in school.
Tonight was the night
he would graduate
from high school.
In the fall,
he would start college.
He was the best student
in his high school class.
He would give
the class speech.

Rosetta and Vito
dressed up
for the big night.
They sat
in a large room
with the other parents.
They watched
as Dominick
walked to the front
of the room.

He wore
a black gown
and a broad, flat hat.

Dominick stood
before the crowd
and began his speech.

"Mamma and Papa
came from Italy,"
he began.
"They had seven children.
They have worked hard.
Every one of us
has finished high school!
Mamma and Papa
are good and simple people.
They want nothing more
than to see their children
do well in the world.
I am so glad
that my parents
came to America.
We must all
thank our parents."

Rosetta wiped away
her tears.
"Such a good boy,"
she whispered to Vito.

Vito took her hand.
"All of our children
are good children,"
he whispered back.
"Thanks to you."

"Thanks to you too!"
Rosetta smiled.

Then the whole crowd
clapped their hands
for Dominick.
Everyone stood up.
Rosetta and Vito
were bursting with pride.
They looked at each other,
smiling and clapping.

At home that night,
Rosetta and Vito
sat down together.

"Our children
have moved past Little Italy.
Maybe now is the time
for us to move on too,"
said Vito.

"Little Italy
is fine with me,"
said Rosetta.
"My friends are here.
This is my home."

And so they stayed
in Little Italy.
So many years
had gone by
since Ellis Island.
Seven children
had grown up.
Rosetta and Vito
were not young.
They were not rich.

But their dreams
had come true.
Their hard work
and hard times
had paid off.
They had given their children
a better life.
The gift
of a better life
for their children
was all they ever wanted.

Glossary

Definitions and examples of certain words and
terms used in the story

Chapter 1 – Hard Times in Italy page 1

shaking — Moving something rapidly to
and fro, back and forth.
...shaking his head from side to side.

rubbing — Moving one's hand back and
forth over a surface; here, his head.
*"No, no, not that," said Vito, rubbing his
head.*

wearing out (to wear out) — To be used a
lot and become less useful or strong.
And our land is wearing out.

make a better living — To improve one's
life, such as having more money and better
things.
"We could make a better living," said Vito.

Chapter 2 – A Ship to America page 6

hugged (to hug) — To hold someone closely.
They kissed and hugged.

dock — The place where ships are tied.
On the dock he bought a book.

mate — An officer on a ship.
A ship's mate tied a little tag ...

ramp — A walkway with no steps for going into a ship or building.
The ship's mates pushed the people up a ramp.

board — To get on a large vehicle such as a bus, plane, or ship.
The ship's mates pushed the people up a ramp to board the ship.

Chapter 3 – New York page 11

lifted (to lift) — To pick something up.
He lifted them into place.

chicken — Afraid to do something or take a chance.
"It's easy money! Are you chicken?"

(to) bet — To take a chance to get some money by playing a game; gambling.
"I don't want to bet any money," Vito told him.

Chapter 4 – Two Bags page 18

kitten — A baby cat. Also used for a
(usually female) child.
"You don't remember him, do you, my kitten?"

Chapter 5 – Across the Ocean page 22

packed — Very crowded.
The ship was packed full of people.

deck — The upper surface of a ship where
people can work, sit, and walk.
"Take a walk up on the deck."

dust — Very small pieces of matter that can
fly in the air.
"Maybe some dust flew into my eye."

flew (to fly) — Moved through the air.
"Maybe some dust flew into my eye."

Chapter 6 – A New Day page 25

prayed (to pray) — To ask for help from God.
Rosetta had prayed day and night.

clapped (to clap) — To hit one's hands together sharply and produce a noise. It is done to show positive feelings.
Everyone on board clapped and cheered.

cheered (to cheer) — To show positive feelings by using one's voice. Common cheering words are Yea! and Hurray!
Everyone on board clapped and cheered.

spot (to spot) — To see.
Rosetta was the first to spot land.

torch — A thing that holds fire and can be used to give light. (The Statue of Liberty holds a torch high above her head.)
The huge lady held a torch of fire.

crown — Something worn on the head to show someone is important. It is usually circular.
The sun made her crown shine.

pulled into (to pull into) — To arrive, especially at a terminal or other parking spot.
The ship pulled into a large dock.

rush out — To leave in a hurry.
"Don't rush out!" a man called …

check (you) over — To examine; inspect a
person.
They will check you over.

Chapter 7 – Ellis Island page 30

eyelids — The eyes' coverings that can be
open or closed.
She lifted Mrs. Santo's eyelids...

hook — A metal tool that curves at the end
like the thing that is used to catch a fish.
*She lifted Mrs. Santo's eyelids with a long
hook.*

papers — Forms and/or important
documents.
He gave her some papers.

Chapter 8 – Together Again page 36

make do — To do the best one can in a
situation that may be difficult.
We will make do with what we have.

fire escape — Metal stairs on the outside
of a building to be used if there is a fire in
the building.
*...the family went out and sat on the fire
escape.*

Chapter 9 – Mulberry Street page 40

carts — Containers with wheels, often used to carry food; often called pushcarts.
Men pushed carts through the street ...

picked out (to pick out) — To select; choose.
Rosetta picked out oranges.

go bad — To spoil; become unusable.
She didn't want anything to go bad while she talked ...

Chapter 10 – Building a Life page 44

handed down — Reused, like clothes that were used by older children and then used by younger ones.
The old clothes were handed down from one child to the next.

torn — Damaged; ripped.
Dominick came home from school with torn pants.

Chapter 11 – Lucky To Be Alive page 49

board — A long, flat piece of wood.
He stood on a board near the top of the building.

load — Several things that are carried together like a package and delivered somewhere.
"Two more loads!" shouted the boss.

grab (to grab) — To quickly catch and hold something.
Vito tried to grab a rope.

rope — A thick, strong string.
Vito tried to grab a rope.

slipped (to slip) — When a foot does not hold its place on something like the floor, and often causes someone to fall.
His foot slipped.

watch out — Be careful; pay attention; danger!
"Watch out!" he heard someone say.

pile — Several things collected together, often with things on top of other things; a heap.
He landed … on a pile of stones.

for dear life — Desperately; saving oneself from danger and hurt.
He just held on to the rope for dear life.

Chapter 12 – **Paper Flowers** page 54

to make something of your life (lives) —
To be successful.
*"I want you to make something of your
lives."*

Chapter 13 – **Festa!** page 57

festa — Italian word for festival.
Summer was time for the church festa.

pinned (to pin) — To attach something
using a small pointed metal tack or nail.
They pinned dollar bills to the church door.

set off (to set off) — To light and cause to
explode.
After dark they set off fireworks.

fireworks — Things that explode into
striking shows when lighted by a flame.
After dark they set off fireworks.

Chapter 14 – Top of the Class page 61

dressed up (to dress up) — To put on one's best clothes.
Rosetta and Vito dressed up for the big night.

wiped (to wipe) — To clean; often using the hand like a brush to sweep something away.
Rosetta wiped her tears.

whispered (to whisper) — To speak very softly.
"Such a good boy," she whispered to Vito.

bursting — In this case, full of pride, very proud.
Rosetta and Vito were bursting with pride.

paid off (to pay off) — to result in success.
Their hard work and hard times had paid off.